Rapunzel

Illustrated by John Kurtz

JUMP AT THE SUN/HYPERION BOOKS FOR CHILDREN

New York

Text copyright © 2007 by Jump at the Sun

Illustrations copyright © 2007 by John Kurtz

Printed in the United States of America
First Edition
1 3 5 7 9 10 8 6 4 2

This book is set in 18/24 Cantoria MT.
Library of Congress Cataloging-in-Publication Data on file.
ISBN 0-7868-5653-X

Visit www.jumpatthesun.com

Zoe Derenoncourt

Once upon a time . . .

"J"ma + Pop Pop

. . . long, long ago, there lived a man and woman who were waiting for their child to be born. The woman longed for the sweet taste of rampion, a small turnip, which grew miles away in another kingdom.

One morning, the man set out to get some rampion for his wife. Later that day, he came upon a garden of flowering rampion! But the garden was surrounded by a wall of stone.

Now, those who lived nearby never dared to go into the garden. It was owned by an evil witch. But the man did not know this and climbed the wall. He picked a handful of rampion and took it home to his wife.

His wife was very happy. She ate it right away. But the next day she craved rampion again. So her husband went back and gathered twice as much as the day before.

The man went to the garden every day for a week. One day, he heard a voice:

"How dare you come into my garden and steal my rampion! You will pay for it!"

The man explained that his pregnant wife craved rampion.

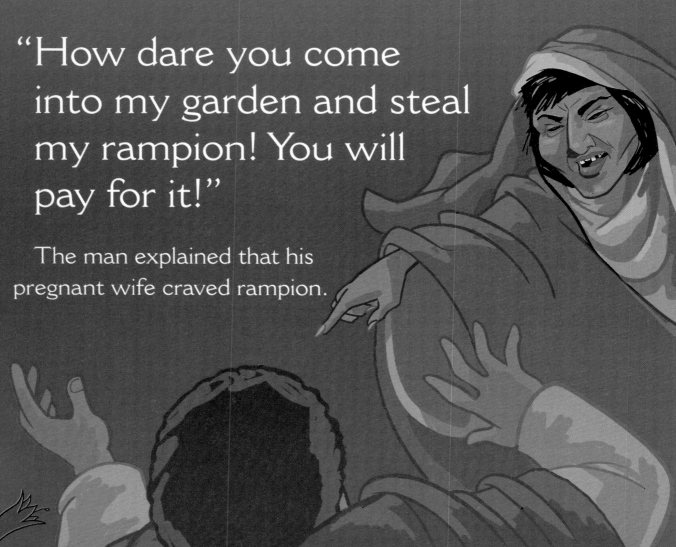

A witch appeared! "Hmmm . . . you and your wife are expecting a child?" she said. "Well, then, you may continue to take the rampion to her, but once your child is born, you must give the child to me, or you and your wife will die!"

Frightened, the man sadly agreed. That night, even the rampion didn't please the woman. They could not bear the thought of losing their child.

One day, the king's son was riding through the forest. He heard a beautiful song and followed the voice to the tower.

Just then, he saw the witch and heard her cry:

Rapunzel, Rapunzel,
Let down your hair to me.

Then the witch climbed Rapunzel's beautiful hair up the tower.

The next day, the king's son returned to the tower. He called out:

Rapunzel, Rapunzel,
Let down your hair to me.

Rapunzel let down her hair. When the prince entered the tower, Rapunzel gasped, "Who are you?"

Rapunzel softened when he told her of his love for her singing.

The king's son returned each day for a month, and Rapunzel's fondness for him turned to love. One day he asked Rapunzel to marry him.

"Yes, but I cannot get down from this tower of stone. If you bring me silk each day, I will weave a ladder," she said.

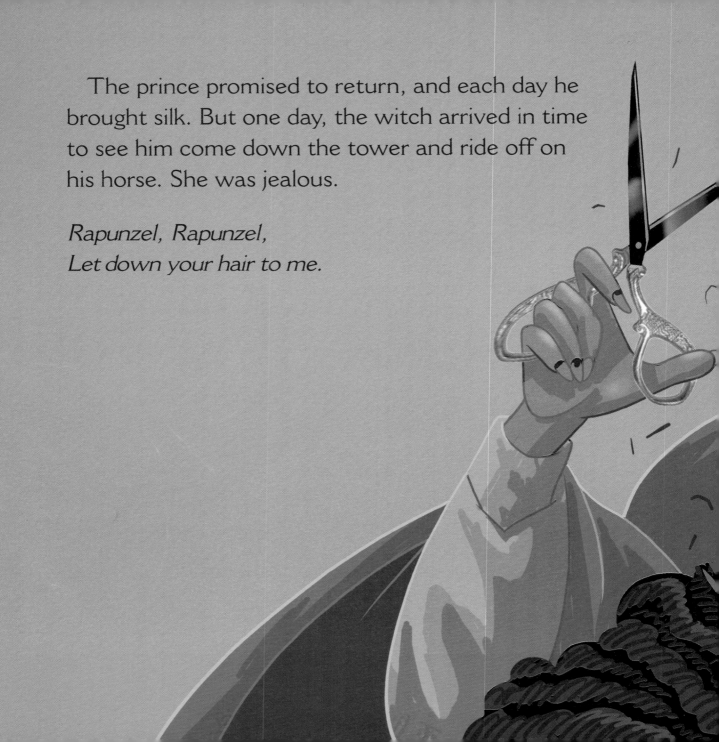

The prince promised to return, and each day he brought silk. But one day, the witch arrived in time to see him come down the tower and ride off on his horse. She was jealous.

Rapunzel, Rapunzel,
Let down your hair to me.

Rapunzel let down her long, thick hair, and the witch climbed up the tower. The witch cut off Rapunzel's beautiful braids, dragged her back down with a long rope hidden in her cape, and banished Rapunzel to the desert to live out her days alone.

The next day, the prince returned with the songbirds, who had woven a ladder of rampion and silk as a surprise. The prince called out:

Rapunzel, Rapunzel, let down your hair to me.

This time, the jealous witch lowered
Rapunzel's braids.

"I tried to protect Rapunzel. You will never
see her again!" she cried. The prince was so
frightened he jumped from the tower into a
thorn bush and was blinded.

Rapunzel wandered the desert for a year and, because her life was enchanted, she was able to give birth to twin boys to keep her company. Every day she sang sweet melodies in their ears to calm them.

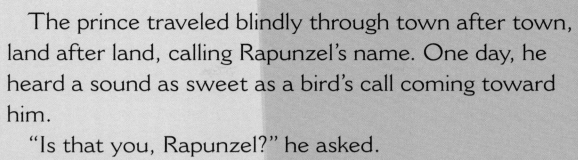

The prince traveled blindly through town after town, land after land, calling Rapunzel's name. One day, he heard a sound as sweet as a bird's call coming toward him.

"Is that you, Rapunzel?" he asked.

"It is I," she said, and cried tears of joy, which fell into his eyes and washed the cursed thorns away.
    The prince regained his sight, and he, Rapunzel, and the two boys lived happily ever after.